Mermaids
TO THE RESCUE

Cascadia Saves the Day

Lisa Ann Scott

illustrated by
Heather Burns

SCHOLASTIC INC.

Text copyright © 2019 by Lisa Ann Scott
Illustrations by Heather Burns, © 2019 Scholastic Inc.

All rights reserved. Published by Scholastic Inc., *Publishers since 1920*. SCHOLASTIC and associated logos are trademarks and/or registered trademarks of Scholastic Inc.

The publisher does not have any control over and does not assume any responsibility for author or third-party websites or their content.

This book is a work of fiction. Names, characters, places, and incidents are either the product of the author's imagination or are used fictitiously, and any resemblance to actual persons, living or dead, business establishments, events, or locales is entirely coincidental.

ISBN 978-1-338-26705-1

10 9 8 7 6 5 4 3 2 1   19 20 21 22 23

Printed in the U.S.A.   40

First printing 2019

Book design by Yaffa Jaskoll

To Talia, for diving in deep!
Thanks for all your help.

Chapter 1

Merfolk of all ages filled Ocean Tides Park, working on sandcastles and sculptures. Crews from the kingdom of Astoria set up amusement rides while vendors stocked their carts and stands with treats and sweets.

"This is going to be the best Sand Sculpture Festival ever!" Princess Cascadia said to her younger sister, Princess Nixie. Cascadia had volunteered to organize the festival this year. She had already graduated from the

Royal Mermaid Rescue Crew School, so she didn't have to attend Rescue Crew classes on the weekend and had plenty of time to plan the event.

Mermaids from across the Eastern Kingdoms were flocking to Astoria City for the biggest, most exciting event of the year.

School was canceled for a week so they could enjoy the festival.

"What do you think of my seapony sculpture?" Nixie asked. "I've been working on it for three days!"

Cascadia smiled at her sister. "I can't believe you made it yourself."

"I bet you win a prize for sure," said Cascadia's seapony partner, Periwinkle.

Nixie blushed happily. "That would be amazing! But I have a little more work to do."

Gorgeous sculptures were scattered throughout the park. And right in the middle was a huge sandcastle. Everyone at the festival could add their own shell or special touch to it. It was the centerpiece of the event and would become a permanent feature of the park.

"I hope there's coral candy," Nixie said.

"Mmm. Kelp kones, too," Cascadia said.

"Help!" called out a voice on the rescue shells around their necks. All members of the Royal Mermaid Rescue Crew wore one to answer calls for help around the Eastern Kingdoms.

Cascadia picked up her shell. "This is the Rescue Crew. What's the emergency?"

"A whirlpool is tearing up my front yard," said a voice through the shell.

"A whirlpool?" Cascadia shook her head like she was hearing things.

"I didn't make it!" Periwinkle laughed. "I've been with you the whole time." Periwinkle's sea savvy was conjuring small whirlpools.

"I know it wasn't you." Cascadia frowned. "But I've never heard a call for a whirlpool before." Surely, this was a mistake. She spoke into her shell. "Where are you?"

"The conch homes, on the south side."

"I'll be right there," Cascadia replied.

Nixie looked worried.

"I'm sure it's nothing," Cascadia assured her. "We'd know if a whirlpool had swept through. They're very rare."

"I should come with you," Nixie said.

Cascadia shook her head. "I can handle this myself. Have a good time finishing your sculpture."

Nixie smiled. "Thanks. You're the best big sister."

Cascadia and Periwinkle swam to the rows of shell homes just outside the city. An older mermaid was waiting on her porch. Cascadia recognized her from many other calls. Mrs. Sherkston was the type to worry. One time she thought a ghost was in her

oven. It was a hermit crab. Another time she thought someone had stolen her purse, but it was on her shoulder!

"What's wrong, Mrs. Sherkston?" Cascadia asked.

"Thank goodness you're here," Mrs. Sherkston said. "This tiny spinning monster whooshed through my front yard and left such a mess!" The seagrass in her front yard was indeed torn up.

Cascadia smirked, suspecting the tiny spinning monster was actually a rambunctious young merkid, excited for the festival.

Mrs. Sherkston clenched her hands. "It was a whirlpool, I tell you! Haven't seen one of those since I was a child. Could mean a big storm is coming."

"Well, it doesn't look like anyone else's yard was hit," Cascadia said. "And I don't see a whirlpool anywhere now. No one else has called one in. I think everything is safe. I'll ask someone from the city to come over and repair your yard once the Sand Sculpture Festival is over. Everyone's busy working on that."

The merlady frowned. "I hope the whirl-pool doesn't come back while everyone is focused on sandcastles."

Cascadia patted her hand. "It won't. Now be sure to come down to the festival tomorrow."

"I'll do that," Mrs. Sherkston said. "Thank you, dear, for coming to check on me."

"That's what the Royal Mermaid Rescue Crew is for!" Cascadia said with a smile.

She and Periwinkle swam back toward the city.

"Hopefully, that monster doesn't attack any other yards!" Periwinkle laughed.

Cascadia laughed, too. But deep down, something was bothering her. Like a tin-gling feeling telling her something wasn't right. Cascadia shook off her worries. She wasn't going to let this ruin her great day.

When they reached the park, Cascadia gazed at the beautiful sand sculptures. Everyone was laughing and smiling.

"I'm so excited to be part of this!" she cried.

"You've done a wonderful job," Periwinkle said.

Cascadia swam home bursting with pride.

"Sounds like the festival is going to be amazing!" her dad, King Zale of Astoria, said as they ate dinner.

"Good work, honey," said her mom, Queen Avisa.

"I can't wait to ride the seapony carousel," Nixie said.

"I'm going to eat all the seaweed cakes," said Rip, Nixie's seapony partner.

"How did that rescue turn out?" Nixie asked.

"It was another false alarm from Mrs. Sherkston." Cascadia laughed and told them the story. "I hope I find out which little rascal gave her such a scare."

Rip frowned. "How do you know she was wrong? What if it really was a small whirlpool? Small whirlpools are a warning sign that a big undersea storm is on the way. I read about it in *Natural Disasters of the Seas*."

Cascadia felt that little tingling feeling

again. But she crossed her arms. "I'm sure she was confused. No one else reported anything strange."

"There wasn't much damage at all," Periwinkle added.

King Zale chuckled. "I remember responding to calls from Mrs. Sherkston when I was a new Rescue Crew member."

His seapony partner, Storm, bobbed his head. "We were there many times and never for anything serious."

Cascadia raised her chin. "It was just another false alarm."

"I hope you're right," Rip said.

"I'm sure I'm right," Cascadia said. And she *was* sure.

Mostly.

Chapter 2

Cascadia tossed and turned that night. Whirlpools swirled through her dreams. She even heard someone scream.

"Wake up!" Her mom was shaking her shoulders.

Cascadia sat up and rubbed her eyes. "What's wrong?"

"A giant whirlpool is headed for the city. We need to get in our underground sea cave."

"What?"

"A whirlpool. Come on!" Her mom reached for her hand and led Cascadia to the cave below the castle where Nixie clung to their dad.

The family's seaponies huddled in the corner.

Cascadia's heart raced. Tears pricked her eyes.

"Don't worry, dear; we'll be safe down here," her dad said.

That worried feeling sat like a big lump in her stomach.

"I could have warned everyone yesterday when Mrs. Sherkston told me she saw a tiny whirlpool," Cascadia said. She took a deep breath. "But I didn't believe her."

Her mom put her arm around her. "Honey,

we haven't had a storm like this in decades. No one could have known."

"There are usually *many* reports of tiny whirlpools before a big one hits," her dad said. "You heard of only one. From a mermaid who makes lots of mistaken reports."

Cascadia hung her head. "But when we left, I had this feeling deep down that something wasn't right. And I ignored it." She sighed. "Maybe there were other sightings but no one reported them. I should have asked around. I should have investigated the possibility."

"Then we'll consider this a good lesson to listen to those deep-down feelings," her mom said. "But there's nothing you could have done to stop this."

"It's going to be okay." Nixie crossed her

arms as their mother comforted Cascadia. "Once the storm passes, the Rescue Crew can help everyone who needs it."

Rip nodded. "We'll be ready for anything."

"I know only how to conjure a whirlpool," Periwinkle grumbled. "I wish I knew how to stop one, too."

"Help! My roof just disappeared!" cried a voice over the royal family's rescue shells.

"We've got to go make sure they're okay!" Cascadia raced to the door.

Her mom shook her head. "It's too dangerous for anyone to be out there until the storm passes. That includes the Rescue Crew members. If we get injured, who's left to help?"

"She's right," said her dad.

"This is the Rescue Crew. We're sorry," Cascadia's mom said into her shell. "It's too dangerous to respond right now. Seek shelter in your sea cave. We'll be there as soon as the storm is over."

Cascadia wrapped her arms around herself as she listened to the storm howl outside. She shivered, even though she wasn't cold.

"I hope it misses the park," Nixie said.

Cascadia's stomach turned. She hadn't even thought of that!

"Help! My door blew off!" cried another voice from their shells.

"We'll be out when the storm passes," their dad told the frantic mermaid.

Nixie's teeth chattered and her eyes were wide. "How long do these storms last?"

"I've never experienced one," her father said.

"From what I've read, most whirlpools pass through an area quickly," Rip said. "Perhaps fifteen minutes. But sometimes slow-moving storms can linger for up to an hour."

Cascadia didn't think she could bear to

listen to the shrieking, swirling water much longer.

As they waited, more rescue calls came in. "Luckily, none of these calls are for injuries," Cascadia's mom said.

"It's going to be a busy day," Periwinkle said.

"The Rescue Crew can handle it. We must handle it. The subjects of our kingdom will be counting on us," King Zale said.

Nixie raised her hand. "On my honor, I will be brave as I keep our seas and subjects safe." That was the Rescue Crew motto, and they all took the oath very seriously.

The family sat in silence for a while as the storm blew through the city.

Then Periwinkle said, "Listen!"

"It's quiet," Rip said. "The storm must have passed."

"I think it's safe to take a look," the king said.

Cascadia reached for Nixie's hand as they left the cave and swam out of the castle.

The waters were just starting to brighten as the sun rose above the ocean. It took a moment for Cascadia's eyes to adjust. All around their castle, coral and sea plants were blown about. Some shells had been stripped off the sides of the castle.

"It's not as bad as I feared," her dad said.

Then the calls started coming in again. "I'm missing my pet snail!" cried one mermaid.

"My fence is gone!" someone else cried.

"Is it safe to come out?" asked another.

Cascadia was desperate to see what damage had been done to the park, but she knew they had to help the residents of the kingdom first.

"We should ask all the Rescue Crew members who are here for the festival to meet," she said to her family. "We'll come up with a plan to help everyone."

"Excellent idea," the queen said.

Chapter 3

All the kids from the Rescue Crew School were in town with their parents, too, so there would be lots of hands to help.

"I can't believe this," Lana said as the Rescue Crew members started arriving.

"We peeked out the window as it was sweeping into town!" Cali said.

"I never thought I'd see a whirlpool," Cali's twin, Cruise, said. "We called back home. It didn't hit our kingdom."

"It didn't hit Glister Kingdom, either," said Princess Meri, whose family had come down from the Northern Seas.

"Thankfully, it appears it only touched down in Astoria," Cascadia's mom said.

"We can all help with rescues and repairs," King Keel of Stillwater Kingdom said.

Cascadia's dad had made a list of all the calls that had come in. "It's going to be a long day."

The adults swam off to some of the more serious calls, like missing roofs. The merkids were assigned to simpler calls.

"I'll answer the calls from the conch homes to the south," Cascadia said. She'd have to swim across the park to get there. She was anxious to see if the storm had done any damage to the sand sculptures and festival setup.

"I'll come with you," Nixie said. "And this time, I won't take no for an answer!"

Cascadia was glad to have her little sister coming along. Swimming as fast as she could, she headed toward the park. What she saw made her shoulders slump. Her eyes filled with tears.

"Oh no!" Nixie cried.

Cascadia was too upset to say anything. All of the sculptures had been destroyed. Even the big centerpiece. The rides had toppled over. The carts of food and treats were

missing. "It's ruined. It's all ruined, and it's my fault!"

Nixie touched her arm. "This isn't your fault. No one could have stopped this."

"It's true," Rip said. "You can't stop a whirlpool storm."

"Maybe some of it can be fixed," Periwinkle said.

"But this all took so long to set up!" Cascadia said.

"We can't stop to think about that now," Rip said. "We need to respond to all of these rescue calls."

Cascadia nodded and concentrated on one of the Rescue Crew sayings: *Breathe, focus, solve.* "You're right. Let's go, and we'll come back here when we're done."

They swam off to help merfolk looking for missing things or needing help with minor damages.

Cascadia finished her last call and realized she wasn't far from Mrs. Sherkston's house.

She swam over and saw the mermaid outside, cleaning bits of broken coral off her lawn.

Mrs. Sherkston looked up. "I told you I saw a whirlpool."

Cascadia bit her lip. "I'm sorry I didn't believe you. I just never thought something like this could happen."

"Thankfully, they don't happen often. We'll be all right," Mrs. Sherkston said. "It'll just take some time to clean up."

"Do you need any help?" Nixie asked her.

"No, dear, I'm sure you've got more important things to do than help tidy up my yard."

Like fixing the festival, Cascadia thought. "I'm glad you're okay," she told Mrs. Sherkston. "Come on, guys. Let's go back to the park and get to work."

They zoomed through the water toward the park. When they got there, the adult members of the Rescue Crew were surveying the scene.

Cascadia swam up to her parents.

"What a shame," her mom said, looking around.

"Or a blessing," her dad said.

"What do you mean?" Cascadia asked angrily. "The storm destroyed everything set up for the festival. That's not a good thing."

"I know," her father said. "But it seems the park took the greatest hit. All of the sculptures probably helped break up the whirlpool, so it wasn't as dangerous when it reached the homes outside the city."

"But the festival is ruined!" Cascadia wailed. "It's going to take forever to fix all this."

No one said anything.

Cascadia looked around, wondering why all the adults were so silent. "What?"

"We were discussing the festival just as you arrived," Cascadia's mom said softly.

"There are still many repairs to make around the city. And we need to check the rest of the kingdom, too. There could be animals who need our help." Her dad paused. "So we've decided to cancel the festival."

Chapter 4

"**N**o!" Cascadia cried. "We can fix this. We can work all day and night, and it'll be ready in a few days. Everyone planned to stay in town for the whole week. We can get it ready by the last day at least."

Her mom reached for Cascadia's hand. "Sweetheart, I know this is important to you. But we have to spend our time working on more important things."

Cascadia pulled her hand away. "Then

let me try to fix this. It's my fault it got destroyed. I should have warned everyone a whirlpool had been spotted. Maybe we could have protected the park somehow." She wiped away the tears spilling down her cheeks. This was the worst day of her life!

"Usually, I can swish a fix for anything," Nixie said softly. "But not this time. I spent days on my sculpture, and it's just . . . gone."

Cascadia's shoulders slumped. Her sister, Nixie, was well known for her creative solutions to problems. And now even Nixie was giving up.

Breathe, focus, solve.

"Even if you wanted to rebuild all the sculptures, the whirlpool blew away the extra sand," Princess Lana said. "Do you know how long it would take to collect enough sand and shells to remake everything?"

"We can just redo the centerpiece sculpture, then," Cascadia said. "And we can set the rides back up and all the carts."

No one said anything.

"Come on, there's always a way," Cascadia

said. "We never back down on rescue calls. We always find a way to make things right."

"But this is different," Princess Cali said quietly.

"Cleaning up from the storm is more important than the festival," Prince Cruise said.

"The festival is important, too! Merfolk from all over the Eastern Kingdoms are here to celebrate," Cascadia cried. "Won't any of you help me?"

"It's just too much," Cruise said. "It can't be done."

Cascadia raised her chin. "Then I'll do it myself. By next weekend before everyone leaves, I'll have the festival up and running. Can I try, Mom and Dad? Please?"

Her parents looked at each other. "We have enough Rescue Crew members to cover all the calls," her dad said. "So yes, you may try."

"But don't be too disappointed if you can't get it all done," her mom said.

Periwinkle gave her a sad look. "I'll help you, but I'm not sure we can really do it."

"Yes, we can." Cascadia started gathering debris strewn across the park.

"Well, good luck," said Lana as the rest of the Rescue Crew swam off.

Nixie stayed. "Rip and I will help."

Teary-eyed, Cascadia hugged her sister. "I knew you would."

"We'll start collecting a pile of shells for the sculpture," Nixie said.

While Nixie and Rip dashed off searching for shells, Cascadia and Periwinkle spent the day clearing the park of debris. Periwinkle conjured a few small whirlpools, which swept up a lot of the trash. Then they hauled it outside the city. Crews would throw it all in the rift when they were done.

Merfolk rarely went to the rift. Who knew what was down there! Nixie and Rip had rescued Nixie's friends from the edge of the rift and outsmarted a shark! But luckily, they were able to stay out of the dark, creepy abyss.

The rift had appeared hundreds of years

ago when a great sea storm cracked open the floor of the great ocean, dividing the Eastern and Western Seas. No one knew what was down there, but there were lots of scary theories, like sea monsters and evil mermaids.

That long-ago storm had also blown away the mermaids' magical protective force: a trident holding the Night Star, the Fathom Pearl, and the Sea Diamond. For hundreds of years, the powerful trident had kept the Eastern Kingdoms safe. Shortly after it disappeared, the Royal Mermaid Rescue Crew was formed as guardians of the kingdoms.

"I'm glad we don't have to haul the debris to the rift," Cascadia said.

"Yeah, that place gives me the creeps," Periwinkle said.

They worked through the day without taking any breaks. Cascadia was disappointed no one else stopped to help them. This just made her all the more determined to make sure she could fix the festival. Just her and Nixie and their seaponies.

They worked until the sun set above the seas. "Tomorrow, we'll have to bring some glow coral so we can work into the night." Cascadia's muscles felt sore from all the work. She wasn't sure she'd be able to work late tomorrow—but she had to try.

Nixie groaned. "Okay."

Cascadia paused to look over their progress so far. "That's a nice-size pile of oyster shells you collected. Tomorrow, search for some of those pretty pink ones. Those look great in the sculptures."

"Sure. Most of them are on the outer edges of the kingdom, but we'll find some," Rip said.

Nixie looked around the park. "How are we going to get the rides set up again?"

"I don't know," Cascadia said. "But we'll come up with a plan."

Chapter 5

The next morning, they swam right to Ocean Tides Park.

"Look at this!" Periwinkle hurried over to the oyster shells they'd collected. There was a small pile of pink shells next to it. "Those weren't here when we left last night."

Cascadia picked one up. "Who put them here?"

Nixie shrugged. "Everyone was exhausted

from all the rescues. I can't imagine anyone was collecting shells."

Cascadia put her hands on her hips. "We should gather some more. Maybe we'll figure out who did this. They might be willing to help!"

"Let's bring our new Say Shells so we can communicate with any of the creatures we see," Nixie said.

Cascadia, Nixie, and their seaponies swam out of the city with baskets to collect more shells. They found some empty shells just outside the city.

Two dolphins were passing by.

"Excuse me!" Cascadia swam up to them.

The dolphins stopped swimming. "Hello, Princess!"

"Did the storm cause you any trouble?"
Cascadia asked.

"No, we saw a few small whirlpools and
feared a big one could be coming, so we fled
to a safe place," one of the dolphins said.

"We're just coming back to the area now,"
the other dolphin said.

Cascadia snapped her fingers. "I should have checked with some animals when Mrs. Sherkston reported a whirlpool."

"Well, next time you'll know," Periwinkle said.

"I'll make note of that as well," Rip said.

"I hope there isn't a next time," Nixie said. "That was scary."

"How did the city fare?" the other dolphin asked.

"Thankfully, no one was hurt," Cascadia said. "But there was lots of damage throughout the city. And it destroyed our Sand Sculpture Festival."

"Oh no!" said one of the dolphins. "I always enjoy coming to that."

"We're trying to fix everything, and

someone left a pile of pink shells last night," Cascadia said.

"Was it you guys?" Nixie asked.

"No," the first dolphin said. "But we can collect more."

"You do so much for all the creatures in the sea, it would be a pleasure to help you for once," said the other dolphin.

"Why, thank you! Bring as many as you can find to Ocean Tides Park in Astoria City," Cascadia said.

Nixie gave the dolphins some baskets for the shells, and they swam off to search for glow coral. Then they found a few of the missing food carts and brought them back to the park. It was another long day.

As the sun was setting, they brought out

the glow coral so they could keep working. But soon, they were all exhausted.

"I need sleep," Nixie said.

Cascadia yawned and stretched. "Me too. But I still wish I knew who brought those shells last night."

"Maybe it was a sea fairy!" Periwinkle said.

They all laughed.

"Sea fairies aren't real," Rip said.

"Just in case they are"—Cascadia cupped her hands around her mouth to shout—"sea fairy, please bring us sand!"

Laughing, the sisters and their seaponies swam back to the castle and fell asleep the moment their heads hit their pillows.

They slept in later than Cascadia wanted to, but they quickly grabbed breakfast and swam back to the park.

Cascadia's jaw dropped. "No way!"

"What?" Rip asked.

"Look!" Cascadia pointed to a small pile of sand next to the shells.

"Maybe sea fairies are real!" Nixie said.

Chapter 6

"**S**o what should we do?" Periwinkle asked. "Go look for sea fairies?"

Rip rolled his eyes. "I promise it's not sea fairies. But let's see if we can find who did this."

Cascadia nodded. "Maybe whoever's doing it can bring more."

They swam out of the city toward the big sandbar.

"It doesn't look like any big scoops of sand are missing," Cascadia said.

Three small whales dove down from the surface. Cascadia waved to get their attention. "Hello! Have you seen anyone collecting sand here?"

"You mermaids were doing that a few weeks ago for your festival," one of the whales said. "But we haven't seen anyone else."

"The whirlpool swept away all our sculptures," Cascadia told them. "And we're trying to rebuild."

"Last night, someone left us a pile of sand," Periwinkle explained.

"But we need tons of sand," Cascadia

said. "We're hoping whoever did it would bring more. Was it you guys?"

One of the whales shook its head. "No, but we can help."

"We could easily scoop up some sand in our mouths and drop it off," said another.

Cascadia clapped. "That would be such a big help."

"And that gives us more time to find some of the lost vendor carts," Nixie said.

"But it still doesn't explain who's been helping us at night," Periwinkle said.

Cascadia raised an eyebrow. "I've got an idea to figure that out."

They spent the rest of the day searching for the lost festival carts and supplies. The whales brought sand. The dolphins arrived with more shells. And somehow a few turtles had heard about the festival and showed up with buckets of sea berries to decorate with and snack on.

"This is almost enough to rebuild the festival, don't you think?" Nixie asked.

Cascadia put her hands on her hips. "We still have to get the rides back in place. And convince the vendors to bring back food and treats to sell. And build the sculptures."

"But you're much further along than I ever imagined," Rip said.

"I'm starting to think we might be able to pull this off!" Nixie said.

Cascadia glanced around, then said loudly, "If only we had sea stars. We'll have to work on that tomorrow. Let's go home."

Nixie gave her a questioning look as they swam to their castle. "What's going on?" she finally whispered.

"We're coming back out tonight to find out who's helping us," Cascadia said.

As the sun was setting, they quietly returned to the park and found places to hide.

Cascadia curled up in a sea tree to keep watch. But at least an hour passed and she didn't see anything.

"Should we go home?" Nixie whispered through the rescue shell.

"No! Let's wait longer." Cascadia was getting stiff from crouching in the branches of the sea tree.

And then she heard something by the piles of sand. Cascadia squinted to see better. It looked like a mermaid, but it was ghostly white and glowing. It dumped out a basket of sea stars. She'd never seen a creature like that before. Was it a sea fairy after all?

Cascadia was so stunned, she fell out of the tree.

That startled the creature, who started swimming away.

"Wait! Please!" Cascadia cried.

Nixie and the seaponies emerged from their hiding places and raced over.

"What's going on?" Nixie asked.

"I found our helper, but they're leaving the park!" Cascadia said. "Grab some glow coral and let's go!"

They chased the spectacular creature through the city.

"Please, wait!" Cascadia cried.

"Who are you?" shouted Nixie.

"We're not going to hurt you!" Rip said.

"Are you a sea fairy?" Cascadia called.

Even though Rip was the fastest seapony around, he couldn't catch the creature, who seemed to be darting off in different directions.

"Where did it go?" Cascadia wondered. They were far outside the city.

The four of them looked around. "It seems to have disappeared," Rip said.

"Look! Something up ahead is glowing," Nixie said.

"It's headed for the kelp curtain," Rip said.

Cascadia gulped. "By the rift."

"How will we get through?" Periwinkle asked. "Conjuring a whirlpool won't help get through the curtain. It'll just tangle up the weeds."

Cascadia turned to Nixie. "How did you guys swim through when you rescued your friends?"

"I used a stick to push it aside." Nixie grabbed a stick from the ocean floor. "Follow me!"

Slowly, they swam through the kelp curtain until they were on the other side.

"Look!" Cascadia pointed at the glowing creature hiding by a coral formation. "Please wait!" Now that they were closer, Cascadia could see it was a mermaid—with flowing fins and glowing scales! "Who are you?"

The mermaid put a finger over her lips like she was saying, "Shh," and swam into the deep abyss beside her.

"She went into the rift!" Nixie cried. "That's too dangerous! Who knows what's down there?"

Rip cleared his throat. "I think *she* knows what's down there."

"How?" Periwinkle asked.

"I bet she lives there," Rip said.

Cascadia couldn't believe what she was hearing. "In the rift?"

"Many sea creatures of the deep have bioluminescent features—that's what makes her glow. It helps them see—and be seen—in the dark waters."

Cascadia shook her head in disbelief. "So there really are merfolk living in the rift. All those tales were true."

"But those tales said the rift mermaids were scary and evil. She was quite nice, helping us," Nixie said.

"But *why* was she helping us?" Periwinkle wondered.

"We're going to find out," Cascadia said.

"How?" Rip asked.

"We're going into the rift," Cascadia said.

Chapter 7

"**A**re we quite sure it's a good idea to swim into the rift?" asked Rip.

"We have to find that mermaid and learn what's down there," Cascadia said.

Nixie bit her lip but said, "We'll be fine if we stick together."

The sisters mounted their seaponies, who swam over the giant gash in the sea-floor and slowly sank into the darkness.

Nixie and Cascadia each held out their hunks of coral, lighting the way. There were jagged cliffs along the edges of the rift.

"Hello?" Cascadia called.

"Is anyone here?" Nixie asked nervously.

"The bottom looks like it's a long, long way from here," Periwinkle said.

As they swam down, unusual creatures rushed past them.

"We're not in Astoria City anymore," Nixie said.

"Hello?" Cascadia shouted.

A faint light was rising from below.

"I wonder if that's her!" Cascadia's heart raced.

Nixie waved. "Hello, we're up here!"

The glowing mergirl zoomed toward

them and whispered, "Shh!" She seemed to be no older than Nixie. And didn't seem very happy.

"Hi," Cascadia said cautiously.

"Come out of the rift," the mermaid said. "You must not be seen."

They followed her back to the seafloor and gathered around the coral formation.

"Who are you?" Cascadia asked.

"My name is Galia," the glowing mermaid said.

"I'm Princess Cascadia of Astoria, and this is my sister, Princess Nixie, and our seapony partners, Rip and Periwinkle."

"Pleased to meet you," Galia said.

"Do you live at the very bottom of the rift?" Rip asked.

"Yes, but our city is carved into the side of the cliffs and on top of giant rocks," Galia said.

"Wow!" Nixie said.

"We've never seen mermaids like you," Cascadia said. "Why did you come to the park?"

"A sea quake damaged our city. Everyone's

busy cleaning up, but they said I'm too young to help," Galia explained. "When one of the elders wondered if the oceans above us had been damaged, I got curious. And when the sun started setting, I came up to explore. That's when I found you guys. But I'm going to be in so much trouble."

"Why?" Periwinkle asked.

"We're not supposed to leave the rift." Galia bit her lip. "There are legends about the evil mermaids who live above."

Everyone else laughed.

"That's not very funny," Galia said. "We had no idea who was living up here."

"We're laughing because we've heard similar tales—about the evil mermaids living in the rift," Cascadia said.

"Oh, we're quite peaceful!" Galia said.

"So are we!" Nixie said.

"How many mermaids live in your city?" Rip asked.

"A few hundred," Galia told them.

"How are repairs to the city going?" Periwinkle asked.

"Slow," Galia said. "There's a lot of damage. More than in your city."

"We better tell Mom and Dad they can't throw all that debris down here like we planned. They're the king and queen of Astoria," Cascadia explained.

Galia smiled. "My parents are king and queen of Meridium."

"So you're a princess, too!" Nixie said.

Galia nodded.

"Since you're already up here, let us show you around the city!" Cascadia said.

"Okay," Galia said. "But be sure no one else sees me!"

Chapter 8

The mermaid sisters and the seaponies led their new friend past the rows of shell homes on the way back to the city.

"These are just the cutest!" Galia said. "I've always dreamed of coming here. It was quite a thrill when I first snuck up."

They swam past Ocean Tides Park, and Periwinkle asked, "If you were trying to sneak around and not be noticed, why did you decide to help us?"

Galia smiled. "Once I realized you weren't evil mermaids, I felt bad that your festival had been ruined. Since I can't help clean up my city, I thought at least I could help you."

"I'm so glad you did," Cascadia said, "or we never would have met you."

Next, they swam toward the Royal

Mermaid Rescue Crew School in the middle of the city. The roof was missing many of its shells, but at least it hadn't been damaged like the homes in the rift, Cascadia thought.

"What is the Royal Mermaid Rescue Crew?" Galia asked.

"All the royal mermaids of the Eastern Seas come here on the weekends so we can learn how to keep our seas and subjects safe," Cascadia explained.

They told Galia about their classes and some of their rescues.

"I wish we had something like that in Meridium," Galia said. "Then maybe my mom and dad would let me help when something important like a sea quake happens."

"I wish you could go to Rescue Crew School with us," Cascadia said.

Galia shook her head. "My parents would never let me spend time with creatures from the surface."

"I don't think we'd be allowed to spend time with creatures from the rift," Nixie said. "It's not fair."

They showed Galia around the rest of the city, and ended the tour with a visit to their castle.

"This is the most beautiful thing I've ever seen!" Galia said.

The water started brightening. "The sun will be rising above the ocean soon," Cascadia said.

"I've got to get home," Galia said.

"Will we ever see you again?" Nixie asked.

Galia sighed. "I don't know."

"I really wish we could help you," Periwinkle said.

Galia shook her head. "My parents can never know I came up here. I'm so mad I can't tell anyone about my adventures with you guys!"

"News of your existence belongs in our textbooks," Rip said. "But I won't say a word, if it helps keep you safe."

Cascadia blinked back tears, knowing there were too many things in the way of them being friends. "Please visit again. Anytime you want to come visit at night, just rap on my window to wake me up."

"I'll try," Galia said. "But I really have to go."

Suddenly, the gates to the castle rose.

Galia hid behind Rip, and the others formed a circle around her.

The king and queen swam out, chatting. They stopped when they saw the merkids and seaponies in front of the castle. "What are you children doing up so early?" the queen asked.

King Zale raised an eyebrow. "Or are you out late?"

"We're working on the festival," Cascadia said quickly.

"You've made tremendous progress," her dad said.

No one said anything.

"What's wrong? What are you four up

to?" Queen Avisa asked. "You're all acting so strange."

"What are you hiding?" the king asked, swimming up to the group. "Let me see."

With a sigh, Cascadia swam away from the group, revealing Galia in the center.

Cascadia's mom gasped. "Who is that?"

Chapter 9

"This is Galia." Cascadia wondered how in the world she was going to explain this.

Galia's eyes widened. "Nice to meet you, but the sun is rising and I have to go!" Galia wiggled out of the circle and dashed off.

"She was—glowing!" Cascadia's mom said.

"Who was that?" her dad asked.

Cascadia and Nixie looked at each other. "A new friend," Cascadia said.

"Then why did she swim off so quickly?" their mom asked.

Their dad crossed his arms. "And why did it matter that the sun is coming up?"

Cascadia wrung her hands in front of her. She wanted to keep Galia's secret, but she didn't want to lie to her parents. "Galia lives in the rift."

"What?" her mom and dad said at the same time.

"We'd know if merfolk lived down there," her dad said.

"They live way down at the bottom," Nixie said.

Cascadia launched into a story about everything that happened: how Galia had

been secretly helping them, how her town had been damaged by a sea quake.

"The sea quake probably caused the whirlpool," her father said.

"I hope they're able to rebuild," her mom said.

"Make sure we don't throw our trash in the rift," Cascadia said.

"Of course not! And we're almost done with our cleanup. We've made great progress here in Astoria," her dad said. "In fact, we're all gathering in the park this morning to discuss what's next."

"Why don't you come with us?" her mom asked. "Unless you need to get some sleep." She raised an eyebrow.

"We'll come!" Cascadia said.

They swam to the park, where many of the older Rescue Crew members were gathering, too.

"So what's left to do?" Cascadia's dad asked.

"We finished repairing the homes on the south side," King Keel said.

"We just need to replace some of the roof shells at the school and we're done there," King Marinus said.

"We're going to be able to finish all that up today," Cascadia's dad said. "But I have one more job I'd like to add to the list."

"What did we miss?" Queen Yara asked.

"The festival," her dad said.

"I thought we canceled the festival?" Queen Nerina asked.

"We did," Queen Avisa said, "but we also told Cascadia she could try to fix everything. And look at how much she and her friends have accomplished!"

Cascadia knew she was blushing with everyone looking at her. "We had some help."

"But you made incredible progress. And

we figure if all of us work with you, we can have the festival after all!" her dad said.

"That would be great!" Princess Meri said. Cruise and Cali shared a high five.

Cascadia knew she should be excited, but something was tugging at her heart. If there were so many crew members to help with

the festival, they should really help the mer-folk in the rift instead.

Cascadia bit her lip and turned to her parents. "Can I talk to you—in private?"

"Sure," her mom said. "Aren't you excited about this?"

"I would be, if there wasn't a more impor-tant job to do," Cascadia said.

"Come tell us." Her father led them away from the crowd.

"Instead of finishing the festival, I think all of us should help the merfolk in the rift. There's so much to do," Cascadia said.

"We've never even been in the rift," her dad said.

"We have," Cascadia said.

"What?" her mother shouted. "When?"

"Last night," Cascadia said. "We had to find out who was helping us, so we followed her there."

"What a risky thing to do!" her mom said.

"I know, but we're fine," Cascadia said. "And they're not. They need our help."

"We don't even know if they'd want our help. What if they consider us enemies?" her dad asked.

"Maybe Galia could bring her parents up to meet you? Then they could see we mean no harm," Cascadia said.

Her mom squeezed Cascadia's shoulder. "I love your kind heart, but I'm not sure this is a rescue we want to take on."

"Why not? We're supposed to keep our seas and subjects safe! The rift is part of our seas."

"You're right," her dad said. "We should try to help."

"Let's meet with them first before telling anyone else about this," her mom said.

"I'll tell the others to finish working on the festival while we go to the rift," her dad said.

Cascadia was so excited. But she was worried, too. What if Galia got in big trouble? What if her parents weren't happy to meet them?

Chapter 10

"I can't believe we're swimming to the rift again," Nixie said.

"We're going here so often these days, we should probably cut a path through the kelp forest," Rip said.

"Did you just make a joke?" Periwinkle teased.

"I was only partly joking," he said as they approached the kelp curtain.

Nixie grabbed a stick and led them through, all the way to the other side and the dark shadow of the rift.

But they didn't get far before they saw several glowing creatures rising from the deep.

"Galia!" Cascadia shouted as they came into view.

Galia swam up to them. "These are my parents, King Finn and Queen Delta." She looked down. "They caught me sneaking home, so I told them everything."

"Nice to meet you," Cascadia said, shaking their hands. "I'm Princess Cascadia. These are my parents, King Zale and Queen Avisa of Astoria, and my sister, Princess

Nixie. And these are our seapony partners, Periwinkle and Rip. And my parents' seaponies, Storm and Kyla."

Everyone greeted each other.

"We were coming to the surface to see if Galia's tales of kind merfolk living up here were true," King Finn said.

"It is true. In fact, we were coming down to see if our Rescue Crew could help repair your city," Cascadia's mom said.

The king and queen looked at each other. "You'd do that for us?"

"We keep our seas and subjects safe. That's the Rescue Crew motto. We help everyone in the Eastern Kingdoms," Cascadia said. Getting the festival up and running no longer seemed important.

"But how will you be able to see?" the queen asked. "We're used to the dark, but you aren't."

Nixie held up a chunk of glow coral. "We'll bring lots of this."

"And we'll be back with lots of help," Cascadia's dad added.

The Rescue Crew members and their seapony partners from across the Eastern Seas headed for the rift, along with the teachers from the Rescue Crew School. They would learn so much about the rift.

Cascadia asked the dolphins, whales, and turtles to help, too.

"But what about your festival?" a whale asked. "You're so close to being done. We were going to help pull the rides back into place today."

"You guys are the best. But this is so much more important," Cascadia said.

One of the dolphins twirled in a circle. "What an adventure! I've never been into the rift."

Galia and her parents were at the top of the rift to greet everyone and lead them to their city.

"This is kind of spooky," Dorado said as they swam into the darkness.

"And I thought swimming to the Northern Seas was an adventure!" Lana said.

"Beat you down there," Cali said.

"Go right ahead!" Cruise said.

They swam down and down until they got to the city of Meridium.

"Everything is glowing!" Nixie said. "It reminds me of our waters just before sunset."

"It's bioluminescent algae," Galia said. "We grow it along the walls to provide some light."

They tossed their glow coral in a pile to create an even greater light. Then they saw the devastation. Caves in the walls were filled with rubble. Some of the homes had toppled off their rock formations. Giant boulders were strewn about. Cracks lined the ocean floor.

"Oh my," King Zale said.

Cascadia stopped swimming and looked around. "This is really bad. Are you going to be able to fix everything?"

Galia shrugged. "Some merfolk are worried we might have to move and start all over again building a new city."

"That's terrible!" Nixie said. "Maybe you can move to the surface and live with us."

Galia shook her head. "We can't tolerate the light for long. We've adapted to the conditions at the bottom of the rift."

Curious glowing merfolk swam out of caves in the wall. "What's going on?" one of them asked.

King Finn explained everything.

One of the rift mermaids crossed her arms. "How do you know we can trust these strangers? We don't know anything about them."

"And they don't know anything about us," King Finn said. "But even so, they're willing to help us."

"And we desperately need their help," Queen Delta said. "Perhaps we won't have to start over after all."

"Let's get to work," Cascadia's dad said.

"Where should we put all the rubble?" Cascadia asked.

"We can dig a hole for you to dump it in," the turtles said, and they got to work using their flippers to clear away the sand.

Periwinkle conjured a few small whirlpools and swept up some of the trash.

Whales used their tails to slap away

rocks from the openings of caves. Everyone was working hard.

On the edge of the city, Cascadia noticed mounds of rocks and bleached coral. "This looks old."

"That's left over from the great storm years ago that created the rift. It's always been there," Galia said.

Cascadia stared at it for a few moments, when something in the old pile of rubble caught her eye. She swam for a closer look, until Dorado said, "Whoa, look at that!"

Cascadia turned around and saw a school of seaponies with long, lacy fins and huge coronets swim by. "You can see right through them!" she said.

Then a ghostly white creature slowly

floated past, morphing into different shapes. Fish blinking into different colors zipped by. Cascadia turned around and around, marveling at everything. Losing the festival was disappointing, but discovering this incredible world definitely made up for it.

"Cascadia!" Galia waved for her to come over.

Cascadia swam to a group of glowing mermaids.

"These are my friends!" Galia said.

The rest of the Rescue Crew students swam over. "Hi!" Cali said.

Galia introduced them to her friends, who had a million questions.

"Is it scary up there?" asked a mermaid named Sabrina.

"Are there dangerous creatures?" asked a merboy named Dylan.

A mermaid named Isla wondered if humans were real.

Cascadia and her friends laughed and

tried to answer the questions as they worked.

King Finn swam into the middle of the crowd. "Let us take a break and feast. Join us in the great hall."

Cascadia was tired and hungry. And she felt a worried tingle deep down. She knew there was something she missed. Something she needed to investigate. But what was it?

Chapter 11

The Meridium merfolk brought out an unusual but delicious soup, and sea-cucumber sandwiches. Fish with long skinny snouts played delightful music as they dined at a table made of whale bones.

King Finn must have noticed the strange looks being shared. "A great number of things find their way down into the rift and we try to make use of them all."

"How long have you lived here?" Cascadia asked.

"Our people have been here since the great storm," King Finn said. "Legend has it that a group of merfolk were trapped down here and adapted over time to the conditions and created our city."

"The great storm changed things for us, too," King Zale said. "It swept away our Trident of Protection, leaving us vulnerable to the dangers of the ocean."

"That's why we have the Royal Mermaid Rescue Crew." Queen Avisa explained how the group was formed.

"But we've found all the missing gems from the trident," Cascadia said.

"We're just missing the trident itself," Principal Vanora added.

"What does it look like?" Queen Delta asked. "We can be on the lookout for it."

"I'll fetch the picture of it back at school," Professor Korla said. "It would be great to have help finding it."

"I'll take you there so we can get back quickly," Rip said. He was the fastest seapony in the history of the Rescue Crew.

The two of them zoomed off, and the Meridian merfolk brought out more food.

Nixie licked her lips. "This is really good!"

"What do you guys eat?" Dylan asked.

Cruise rattled off a long list of his favorite foods.

Cali laughed. "Cruise likes anything, even salty sea urchins."

"I wish we could come to the surface to see your world," said Isla.

"We'd be happy to have you all visit," Cascadia's mom said.

"We can't tolerate the light," Queen Delta said.

"Then visit at night! We have glow coral street lamps," Cascadia said.

"Please, Dad!" Galia begged. "You have to see how awesome Astoria is."

"We were going to have a huge Sand Sculpture Festival, but it's canceled. The whirlpool destroyed everything," Nixie said. "But it would still be fun to visit us."

"But you and Cascadia almost had everything all fixed up!" Dorado said. "All the sand and shells are just waiting there to make new sculptures."

"We came here to help instead," Cali said. "Everyone goes back to their kingdoms tomorrow. There's no time for the festival now."

"Wow, you guys came here instead of going to your festival?" Sabrina asked. "That's really nice."

"You know, we've made such incredible progress here today that I think we all deserve to take a break and have some fun," King Finn said. "We can handle the rest of the cleanup ourselves. Can we come to Astoria right now? It's nighttime; we'll be safe up there."

"Maybe we could all enjoy the Sand Sculpture Festival," Queen Delta said.

"Let's go pull those rides back into place," one of the whales said.

"We'll help!" the dolphins said as they swam off with the whales.

Professor Korla and Rip returned with the painting rolled up. "We brought the gems, too!" Professor Korla said.

Everyone crowded around them for a look.

"I wonder if we'll ever find the trident," Periwinkle said to Cascadia.

"It's been lost for so long that it seems doubtful," Cascadia said.

"Well, we will be sure to look for it. As the king said, a great number of things find their way into the rift." Queen Delta reached out to shake Queen Avisa's hand. "It's the least we can do for helping us."

"It was our pleasure to help, and to make new friends," Cascadia's mom replied. "Now come, join us in Astoria."

"Grab the glow coral outside and let's go!" Nixie said.

As everyone headed out of the great hall, the ground rumbled. A few of the Meridian merfolk screamed.

Cascadia looked at her parents. "What's happening?" She peeked out of the cave.

The ground rumbled again, and the earth started splitting open. A huge gray tentacle slowly slithered up out of the crack.

Cascadia felt like she was back in their sea cave, listening to the whirlpool pass by. She was so terrified she couldn't scream. She couldn't even move!

"Everyone! Back inside the cave walls, now!" King Finn cried.

Chapter 12

The merfolk fled to the main cave, crowding inside. Cascadia heard some of the younger merkids whimpering.

"Wh-wh-what was that?" Nixie asked, her teeth chattering.

Cascadia grabbed her little sister's hand. "I don't know."

"I can only suspect the recent quake has awakened creatures that have been living below us," King Finn said. "Creatures we never knew about."

"There's another one rising from the deep!" shouted a mermaid at the front of the cave.

"What are we going to do?" Galia asked.

"Wait and hope. Hope that they leave," Queen Delta said.

"But what if they don't?" Cruise asked.

"If only we had the Trident of Protection," Rip said.

Cascadia got that tingling feeling deep down again. The same one she'd felt when she answered Mrs. Sherkston's call. The same one she felt when she'd been staring at the old pile of rubble. What had she seen in that pile? The tingling was growing stronger and stronger. This time she wasn't going to ignore it.

She turned to her parents. "Remember when you told me to trust those deep-down feelings inside?" she asked them.

Her mom nodded.

"I can't explain it, but it's telling me I have to go out there." Cascadia zoomed off before they could protest.

Periwinkle followed as she left the cave, and Rip zoomed up behind them with Nixie.

Now three big sea beasts were emerging from the ocean floor, half in and half out of the giant crack.

Cascadia's heart pounded. She had to be fast.

"What are you doing?" Nixie asked.

"I'm certain our textbooks would not recommend this as proper protocol in this situation," Rip said.

"Whoever wrote our textbooks never could have imagined this," Cascadia said. "I have a feeling something's in that pile." She pointed ahead. "Something that can help us." She didn't want to say it out loud to get everyone's hopes up, but she knew now why she'd felt that tingle of worry. "Come on!" She raced to the edge of the city to find the mound.

"What did you see?" Nixie asked as they followed her.

"There was something that didn't seem natural. It seemed mer-made." She swam around the pile looking for it.

And that's when she spotted it again: a triangular tip encrusted in coral. Cascadia reached for it, wiggling her fingers, but couldn't get it.

The ground rumbled again.

"Whatever you're trying to get, you'd better get it quickly," Rip said.

"Periwinkle, can you help?" Cascadia asked.

"Sure thing." She created a small whirlpool that cleared out some of the rocks.

"Is that . . ." Nixie's jaw dropped.

"Oh my goodness!" Periwinkle said.

Rip's eyes widened. "That looks like the missing trident!"

Chapter 13

Cascadia could just reach it. She wrapped her fingers around it and pulled it out. "I sure hope it is."

They raced back to the cave, where her parents waited at the edge of the opening.

"Hurry!" her mother shouted. "Those creatures are almost out!"

"I think I found the trident!" Cascadia held up the heavy staff as she swam back to the door of the cave.

"What?" Astonished, her mom took the staff and scraped away some of the barnacles and coral. Gold gleamed from beneath. "It *is* the trident!"

The crowd gasped and her dad's jaw dropped. "Bring me the gems!" He scraped off the rest of the coral and barnacles, revealing the pure golden staff.

Professor Korla hurried over with the bag of gems.

Her mom placed the Fathom Pearl into one empty space. Her father set the Sea Diamond into another.

Everyone seemed to be holding their breath.

Cascadia's mom handed her the Night Star. "This honor belongs to you."

Cascadia had never felt prouder. She set the Night Star into the last opening. The trident shook in her hand and started to glow. Beams of light shot from it.

Everyone gasped.

"It would appear the protective powers of the trident are restored," Principal Vanora said.

"How does it work?" King Finn asked.

"It repels evil forces nearby," King Zale said.

Cascadia rushed to the front of the cave. The huge beasts were wriggling back into the earth. "It's working! The creatures are leaving!"

As they returned underground, the floor gave way, closing up the cracks in the ocean. Everyone cheered.

"What do we do if they return?" Galia asked.

"They won't. When we restore the Trident of Protection to its rightful place in Astoria City, it will provide a protective force over all the Eastern Seas. Including Meridium," Queen Avisa said.

"Cascadia, they will write about you in history books," Rip said.

Periwinkle smiled at her. "I'm so proud of you."

Nixie nudged Cascadia with her elbow. "Good thing you listened to that feeling this time."

Cascadia was so thrilled she was speechless. She was exhausted from being awake for so long, but there was no way she could sleep anytime soon.

"I'd say it's time to celebrate," King Zale said. "Let's head to Astoria for the festival."

When they reached the surface, it was nighttime above the ocean. But the glow coral in the street lamps cast a soft light that didn't bother the Meridium merfolk and allowed everyone to see.

While they started exploring, Cascadia's dad did something he'd never done before. He made an announcement through his shell to every resident and visitor in Astoria City.

"Attention, merfolk. We have the most exciting news to share. Please meet at Ocean Tides Park in a half hour, where we will make this incredible announcement and celebrate the Sand Sculpture Festival."

Merfolk flocked to the park, whispering and wondering what was going on. Vendors were quickly stocking their carts with food and goodies.

Cascadia's heart was pounding, she was so excited. She still couldn't believe she'd found the trident. And she couldn't believe they were going to have the festival after all! The whales and dolphins had gotten the rides back in place.

Her dad swam to the center of the park and talked through his shell again. "I apologize for interrupting your sleep, but I'm certain you all would want to know that we found the missing trident!" He held it up over his head.

The crowd erupted in applause and cheers.

"Where did you find it?" someone called.

"Who found it?" asked someone else.

"My daughter Princess Cascadia found it in the rift while we were helping the mer-folk of Meridium clean up from a sea quake. Yes, we have friendly neighbors living in the rift."

The glowing merfolk swam into the park.

The crowd gasped.

He did not mention the giant creatures, which Cascadia thought was smart. No need to create a panic, but certainly word would get out soon about what they'd seen.

"Let's celebrate!" Cascadia's dad said. "Build sandcastles, enjoy the rides, meet new friends!"

"And be sure to thank Cascadia for leading the effort to get the festival running," her mom said. "And for leading us to the rift to help our new friends. And for finding the trident. You really saved the day in so many ways."

Cascadia felt so proud that her eyes were filling with tears.

Nixie gave her a huge hug, and merfolk crowded around congratulating and thanking her.

"Come on!" Periwinkle said. "We have to start decorating that sandcastle sculpture!"

Merfolk added shells and unique touches to the huge sculpture in the middle of the park.

"This is the best festival ever!" Cali cried.

"I told you Astoria was awesome!" Galia told her friends.

Even Mrs. Sherkston swam up to add a shell and her signature to the sculpture. Then she turned to Cascadia and said, "Excellent work, Princess. You'll make a wonderful queen someday."

Cascadia blinked a few times. "Thanks." She'd never thought about being the leader of Astoria. But she was sure now she could handle whatever might come her way.

Her mom put her arm around Cascadia's shoulders and hugged her.

"Since we got the trident back, what happens to the Rescue Crew?" Cascadia asked. "Do we still need it?" Cascadia certainly hoped so.

"My dear, our help will always be needed to keep our seas and subjects safe," her mom said. "The trident will just make our job a little easier."

"Thank goodness," Cascadia said. "Because I love being part of the Royal Mermaid Rescue Crew."

Nixie smiled. "Me too."

Cascadia drifted back and looked at

everyone having fun and making friends with merfolk from the rift. She couldn't believe everything that had happened since the whirlpool! Somehow, the worst day of her life had led to the best day of her life.

And she couldn't wait to see what was next.

Welcome to the
ENCHANTED PONY ACADEMY,
where dreams sparkle and magic shines!